For Frieda and Orla,
never parted for long.

First published in 2018 by Alison Green Books
An imprint of Scholastic Children's Books
Euston House, 24 Eversholt Street, London NW1 1DB
A division of Scholastic Ltd • www.scholastic.co.uk
London – New York – Toronto – Sydney – Auckland
Mexico City – New Delhi – Hong Kong

This paperback edition first published in 2019

How to Hide a Lion at Christmas

Helen Stephens

ALISON GREEN BOOKS

It was Christmas Eve, and Iris and her family were getting ready to set off for her Auntie Sarah's. Iris was very excited. "You'll love Christmas!" she said to her lion. The lion had lived with Iris ever since he'd arrived in town, and all the townspeople loved him.

But Mum and Dad said the lion had to stay behind.
"You can't take a lion on a train," said Mum.
"The people in Auntie Sarah's town will
be scared of him," said Dad.

"Not if I hide him,"
said Iris.

She tried squeezing him into her suitcase, but he was too big.

She tried wrapping him up as a present, but he was too wriggly.

She even tried covering him in decorations. But it was no good.

"Poor Lion," said Iris. "He'll be so lonely, all on his own."

"Don't worry. He'll probably just sleep the whole time," said Dad.
"And you can bring your toy lion to keep you company," said Mum.

But Iris was still sad. She hated leaving her lion behind.

The lion didn't like to see Iris unhappy.
So, when the family set off to the train station, he followed them.

Nobody noticed him as he sneaked on to the train,
and found a good place to hide among the luggage.

Iris was looking sadly out of the window. The lion wanted to comfort her.

But, before he knew it, the train had rocked him to sleep.

He was still fast asleep when the family reached their stop and got off the train. Auntie Sarah was there to meet them. "Merry Christmas, Iris!" she said.

But Iris wasn't feeling very merry.
She kept thinking about her lion, all alone at home.

If only she knew!
The lion wasn't at home at all.
He was still on the train, and
heading far, far away
into the night.

When the lion woke up, he was very confused. The train had stopped, and everything was very dark and quiet. Where had everyone gone?

He crept down from his hiding place and tip-toed outside. He looked everywhere for Iris, but there was no one to be seen.

He had to find her
— but which way should he go?

The lion looked back along the railway line. Perhaps if he followed the tracks, they would lead him to Iris?

The snow was
very deep, but he put
one cold paw in front of
the other until at last . . .

. . . he saw a village!

In the main square he saw a huge tree festooned with coloured lights, and people were singing all around it:

Fa-la-la-la-laaaa-la-la-la-laaa!

Perhaps Iris was singing with them?
The lion crept closer.

He found a hat and tried to blend in.
But when he joined in with the singing, it came out as a . . .

and they chased after him, throwing snowballs. Luckily, lions can run fast.

They're good at hiding up trees, too.

As the crowd ran past, the lion noticed something
in an upstairs window. It looked like Iris's toy lion!
Perhaps this was Auntie Sarah's house? He had to be sure,
but how could he check, without waking everyone up?

Just then the lion
saw a funny thing.
A man in a red coat
was climbing up and
down all the chimneys.

Maybe that's how the lion could get inside!

But before he could
even try, there was a huge

WHOOSH!
and a
"HO-HO-HO!"
and the man in the red coat
swooped right over
his head!

The lion slipped.
Then all the snow slid off the roof —

WHUMPF!

— and landed right on top
of him. He couldn't even
move a whisker.

In the morning, Iris woke up
to find a new snowman in the garden.
"That's strange," she thought.

She went outside to have a better look.
It was a very odd snowman. It had a tail.

And when she patted the tail,
it waved at her!

As fast as she could, she scrabbled at
the snow, till she found . . .

. . . her lion!

"You're here!" said Iris.
"It's going to be the best
Christmas ever, now!"

And it was – even if the lion did eat everyone's Christmas dinner.

"Never mind," said Iris . . .

"I prefer pizza anyway!"